GREAT
EXPECTATIONS

CHARLES DICKENS

Editor: Heather Hammonds
Cover Illustration: Catherine Ward
Illustrations: Catherine Ward
Typesetting: Midland Typesetters

Great Expectations
First published in 2008 by
Playmore Inc., Publishers,
58 Main Street, Hackensack, N.J. 07601

The Author
Charles Dickens
(1812–1870)

Charles Dickens, born in Portsmouth, England, was the son of a navy pay office clerk.

When his father was imprisoned for debt, young Charles was sent to work in a blacking factory in London, where shoe cleaner was made. This unhappy part of his life is remembered in one of his most popular books, *David Copperfield.* Later he became a journalist, reporting debates in England's House of Commons.

Soon Dickens began writing stories, many of which were first published in monthly or weekly serial form. These included *The Pickwick Papers, Oliver Twist, Nicholas Nickleby,* and *Great Expectations.*

The wonderful stories Dickens told and the famous characters he created—from Mr. Micawber, Fagin and Mr. Jaggers, to Scrooge, the Artful Dodger, Pip, Magwitch and Smike— have all become part of literary legend.

Contents

Chapter 1

The Convict on the Marsh

It was Christmas Eve, and snow was falling on the Kent marshes near my home, in England. What better time for a seven-year-old boy to rush out and make a snowman?

I ran off to the lonely old church that stood about a mile from our home. I had just entered the churchyard when a huge and terrifying figure rose up from behind a tombstone, right beside me.

I screamed in terror, not knowing who had grabbed me.

"Hold your noise, boy!" the man cried. "Keep still, you little devil, or I'll cut your throat!"

His huge hands now circled my neck. He didn't release his grip until I fell silent, and stopped struggling.

The man was dressed all in gray, and his clothes were soaked and covered in mud. His teeth were chattering, as though he had just run out of the icy sea. He had great leg irons around his ankles, linked by chains. I knew at once that he was a convict. He had probably escaped from one of the old ships now being used as prison hulks at the mouth of the local river, where it emptied into the sea.

"Oh, don't cut my throat, sir," I pleaded in terror. "Pray don't do it, sir."

"Tell me your name, boy," said the man. "Quick!"

"Pip, sir."

"Now, show me where you live," he growled.

I pointed across the marsh to where our small house stood.

Suddenly, the man grabbed me around the waist, tipped me upside-down and emptied my pockets. There was nothing in them except a small crust of bread. He snatched it up and swallowed it greedily.

The man stood me right way up again, but kept me pinned against a nearby tombstone. "Now then, lookee here, boy," he said. "Where's your mother?"

"There, sir," I replied, pointing to another tombstone in a corner of the churchyard. "My father's there too, and my five brothers.

His huge hands now circled my neck.

They're all buried there. Died of the fever, sir. I'm an orphan."

The man's desperate features seemed to soften for a moment, but not for long. "Then who do you live with?" he asked.

"My sister, sir. She's Mrs. Joe Gargery, wife of Joe Gargery, the blacksmith, sir."

"Blacksmith, eh?" he replied, looking down at his legs.

The man pushed me harder against the tombstone and asked a strange question. "Do you know what a file is?"

"Yes, sir," I said. "Mr. Joe uses files to grind iron, in his forge beside our house."

"And is there plenty of food in your house, boy?" he asked.

"The pantry is full for Christmas," I told him.

"Right," he said, threateningly. "You get a file and some food, and bring 'em both back here. And if you don't, I'll have your heart and liver out!"

I was now so frightened that I hung onto the man, in case my shaking legs gave way.

"You bring me that food and the file tomorrow morning," he continued. "And don't you dare say a word to anyone that you have

"Do you know what a file is?"

met me. Do as I say and you'll live. But fail me, and your heart and liver will be torn out and roasted, and eaten! Now you get home and remember every word I've said."

"I w-will, sir. I will," I stuttered. "Goodnight, sir. Goodnight."

I ran off, as fast as I could. After a while, I looked back. The man was still in the churchyard, hugging himself, trying to keep warm.

I raced across the marsh, trying to avoid looking at the gibbet that stood beside the marsh track. Many a thief and scoundrel had been hanged there. I heard the gibbet chains clanking, but I daren't look up. I knew the remains of a pirate were still hanging from it, blowing in the cold wind.

I hurried on home.

Chapter 2
A Thief in the House

Joe, my sister's husband, was standing alone at the front door.

"Where've you been?" he asked. "Mrs. Joe has been looking everywhere for you. She's been on the rampage and she's got the Tickler with her!"

The Tickler was a nasty cane, worn smooth by her using it on me.

My sister, known by most as just Mrs. Joe, was more than twenty years older than me. She had, so they said, brought me up "by hand". In other words, she used that cane on me rather too much.

She was not a good-looking woman. She had black hair and dark eyes, and was tall and bony. She almost always wore a rough apron. Joe was very different. He was short and fair, with blue eyes and blond curls. I loved Joe. He was a mild, good-natured man. We both suffered at Mrs. Joe's hands.

Suddenly, the door burst open. It was Mrs.

Joe. "Where have you been, child?" she cried, striking me with the cane.

I ran past her and into the cottage, taking refuge in the chimney corner. "I've only been to the churchyard," I said, starting to cry.

"Churchyard!" she exclaimed. "If it weren't for me, you'd have been dead and buried in there a long while ago, you ungrateful boy. I've worked so hard bringing you up, I've hardly ever had this apron off since you were a baby. It's bad enough being a blacksmith's wife without having to bring you up too. You two will drive me to the churchyard one of these days, and what a precious pair you'd be without me to look after you."

She stormed out; an event marked by a sudden explosion of gunshot coming from the direction of the prison hulks a couple of miles away. "What's that?" I asked Joe.

"Sounds like they're raising the alarm," he replied. "Another convict must have escaped."

I was sure the alarm was for my convict— the man in the churchyard. That night I hardly slept a wink. I was in terror of the man and I knew that in the morning, I had to rob Mrs. Joe's pantry. If I was caught, I'd have a taste of the Tickler once more.

"Where have you been, child?"

At first light on Christmas Day I got up, and hurried downstairs. Every creaking floorboard seemed to cry out, "Stop thief! Stop thief!"

I opened the pantry door and grabbed the nearest things that came to hand; some bread, cheese, mincemeat, and some rum. I was just about to close the door when I spotted a fine pork pie. I took that too.

After I left the house, I crept into Joe's forge and took one of his files. Then I hurried out onto the marshes. When I reached the churchyard, I saw the man sitting with his back to a tombstone, trying to hide himself from the cold, damp wind racing in from the sea.

I emptied my pockets in front of him. He snatched the bottle of rum and opened it. He took a great swallow, hardly able to hold the neck of the bottle between his chattering teeth. Next, he gobbled down the bread, cheese, mincemeat, and pork pie, all the time looking distrustfully around him.

Every now and then he would stop chewing to listen.

"You haven't brought anyone with you, have you?" he said at last.

"No, sir," I quickly replied. "I hope you're enjoying your food."

Robbing Mrs. Joe's pantry

"Thank you, my boy," he said, "I am."

When he had finished most of the food, he asked if I had brought the file. I gave it to him and he quickly set about grinding through the irons on his legs. "Curse these irons on my sore legs," he muttered.

I saw that both his ankles had bloody sores on them from where the irons had rubbed.

I told him that I had to hurry home before I was missed, but he took no notice and carried on filing. So I walked away. The last I heard of him was when I stopped in the mist to listen. I could still hear the sound of him filing away.

Chapter 3
Christmas Dinner

I fully expected a police constable to be waiting for me when I got home. Not only was there no constable there, but the robbery had yet to be discovered.

Mrs. Joe was busy getting things ready for the Christmas dinner, and she had sent Joe outside to stop him interfering. "And where the deuce have you been?" was her Christmas greeting to me.

I lied and said I had been into the village to hear some carol singing. Our house was about four miles from the village of Cooling.

"Perhaps if I weren't a blacksmith's wife," she replied, "I might have time to listen to carols all day. Now get out of my way. I have things to do."

Each time Mrs. Joe went to the pantry that day, I began to shake with fear. But the hours passed and my criminal activity remained undetected.

At last evening came. Joe was not allowed to take any part in the organization of the dinner. Mrs. Joe did everything, including inviting the guests that *she* wanted to attend. She never invited ordinary folk. She only invited some of the more important members of our village.

They included Mr. Wopsle, the church parson, Mr. Hubble, the wheel maker, and Uncle Pumblechook, who was Joe's uncle.

Joe always said to me that Uncle Pumblechook was the most pompous man he had ever met. But Mrs. Joe liked him because he was an important corn merchant, and had lots of money.

During Christmas dinner, all my sister's guests criticized me.

"I hope the boy realizes how lucky he is to have been brought up by you, Mrs. Gargery," said Uncle Pumblechook.

"Yes, indeed," added Mr. Wopsle.

"Do you hear that?" snapped Mrs. Joe, looking me in the eye. "So just be grateful."

"Why can't the young ever be grateful?" asked Mr. Hubble.

"They are all vicious creatures," said Mr. Wopsle, "especially this young boy."

Getting things ready for Christmas dinner

Everyone at the table, except Joe, mumbled "True!"

"The boy has been a world of trouble to you, hasn't he, ma'am," said Uncle Pumble-chook.

"Trouble!" screeched Mrs. Joe. "I quite often wish he was in his grave, like his brothers."

Toward the end of the meal, my sister proudly announced that she had a special treat for everyone. "You must all taste my pork pie. It is entirely and utterly delicious."

The pork pie! I was sure my crime would be discovered at last. My sister went out to get it. My blood froze. It was now or never. I jumped up from the table and ran for my life.

I had only got as far as the door of the house, when I ran headlong into a party of soldiers with muskets. One of the soldiers, seeing me, held out a pair of handcuffs and said, "Here you are! We'll just put these on, shall we?"

It was several terrifying moments before I realized he was just joking. The handcuffs were not for me.

The sergeant said they were searching for an escaped convict and wanted Joe to repair

I ran for my life.

some handcuffs before they continued the chase. "We're on our way onto the marsh," he explained. "We're pretty sure the convict is out there."

When Joe finished mending the handcuffs, he suggested that a few of us should go down to the marsh with the soldiers and watch the hunt.

Uncle Pumblechook, Mr. Hubble, and Mr. Wopsle all declined the invitation. They said they would rather stay indoors, in front of the fire.

"I'll come!" I cried.

"If you bring the boy back with his head blown to bits," said my sister, "don't expect me to put it together again."

Chapter 4
Captured!

We followed the soldiers across the marsh, to the church.

"I hope we don't find him," I whispered to Joe.

"I don't know who the convict is," muttered Joe, "but I agree. I'd give him a shilling to cut and run whatever he's done."

For my part, I was fearful that if the soldiers did recapture the convict, he would think I had led them to him.

The churchyard was searched and found to be empty. So the soldiers set off farther into the marsh and nearer to the sea. Gradually, Joe and I fell back from them. We even lost sight of them for a while. Then we heard shouts and cries ahead.

We hurried on and came to a deep ditch. Inside it, four soldiers were wrestling with my convict. Water was splashing and blows were being struck. At last the man was overcome, dragged out of the ditch, and handcuffed.

The convict looked over at me. I shook my head, trying to tell him that I was not to blame for the soldiers arriving. He gave no clue that he had even recognized me.

He was marched back to our house, where a cart was brought to take him back to the same prison hulk that he'd escaped from.

Just before he got in, the convict turned and spoke to the sergeant. "I wish to say something about my escape," he began. "It may save someone from being blamed for something that I did."

"You can say what you like," said the sergeant.

"A man, even a convict, must eat," he said. "So last night I came to the house here and stole some food; a bit of cheese, bread, some rum, and a pork pie. I also took a file from the forge, to free my leg irons."

Then he turned to Joe. "I'm sorry I stole your file and I'm also sorry to say, I've eaten your pie. I have to say that it was excellent."

"God knows, you're welcome to it," said Joe, always one of the kindest of men. "We wouldn't have you starved for it, would we, Pip?"

Captured!

At last the man was overcome.

I shook my head and whispered, "No."

The cart moved off, taking my convict and my guilty secret with it.

I was so exhausted that night that I fell asleep downstairs. Joe put me over his broad shoulder and carried me up to bed. I never did tell him the truth about my meeting the convict, and my bold robbery in the pantry. I was too afraid he might think I had done wrong.

So the years passed. But as December came around each year, I always dreaded my sister

"I wish to say something about my escape."

might suddenly announce to Uncle Pumblechook and his chums that I was the true thief
of Christmas past. I remembered that convict
part in fear and terror, and part in thanks that
his confession saved me from Mrs. Joe and her
good friend, the Tickler.

As I grew older, I never completely ban-
ished the image of the convict from my mind. I
wasn't to know that one day, far into the future,
he would find his way back into my life . . .

Chapter 5
A Message from Miss Haversham

When I was about twelve years old I went to work with Joe, learning the skills of a blacksmith. I also went to an evening school in the village. It was run by Mr. Wopsle's sister.

Mr. Wopsle's sister had a daughter called Biddy. Poor Biddy was always such a mess. Her hair needed brushing, her hands needed washing, and her shoes needed mending. The only time she looked tidy was on Sundays, at church.

Biddy and I became great friends, and she helped me learn my alphabet.

"What a scholar you are now," Joe used to say to me.

"Didn't you ever go to school?" I asked.

"Never," he said.

One day I asked Joe how he came to marry my sister.

"I was lonely out here on the marsh," he

Biddy and I became great friends.

explained. "There was just me and my forge. And I was attracted to your sister. She was a fine figure of a woman."

I turned my face away, in case he could see how much I doubted that fact.

"Yes, she is bossy, I must admit," continued Joe. "She likes to keep us in our places, and she does drop down hard on us when she's on the rampage. I wish she didn't take the Tickler to you so often. But, for my sake, perhaps you can overlook her shortcomings."

That evening, my sister went to visit Uncle Pumblechook in the village.

When she got home, she had some news. "Uncle Pumblechook has met Miss Haversham," she announced, "and she asked him to get Pip to go and play at her house. And, as far as I am concerned, if Miss Haversham wants the boy to play there, then the boy will go."

I had heard of Miss Haversham. She was a rich woman who lived alone in the largest house in the village. It was surrounded by a high fence and a locked gate, to keep out robbers.

"How did she come to know of Pip?" asked Joe.

"Uncle Pumblechook moves in higher social

My sister had some news.

circles than you," said my sister. "Remember, he even has his own carriage. He met Miss Haversham and he mentioned Pip to her. She's rich, and who knows, she might become Pip's benefactor. This could be the making of Pip. Anyway, Uncle Pumblechook will be here tomorrow morning to pick him up. He must be polished and shining as never before!"

Later that night, my sister took me into the yard and put my head under the outside water pump. The water was freezing. I was soaped and scrubbed, until I was clean. Afterwards, I was sent straight to bed.

The next morning I was dressed in clean linen and trussed up in my tightest suit.

Uncle Pumblechook duly arrived and I was put aboard his carriage, which then set off toward the village.

As we neared the village, I wondered to myself, "What on earth am I expected to do at Miss Haversham's?"

We eventually reached Miss Haversham's house and I was dropped off near the gate. I rang the bell. A few minutes later, a very pretty young lady appeared from the house, and walked up the path to unlock the gate. She was about my age.

A Message from Miss Haversham

"I'm Pip," I said. "I've come to play."
The girl unlocked the door and ushered me in. "Follow me, boy!" she snapped.

Chapter 6
The Wedding That Never Was

We went into the house by a side door. The first thing I noticed was that although it was still early morning, the whole place was in darkness. The girl had left a candle burning. She picked it up, so that we could find our way up a staircase and down the darkest of passages.

At last we stopped by an imposing door. "Go in, boy," she said. "Miss Haversham is expecting you."

With that, she left me. I was trembling, half afraid to enter the room. At last I got the courage to knock on the door.

"Come in," came a voice.

I entered and found myself in a large room, well lit by candles. No glimpse of daylight was to be seen. I thought it must be a dressing room, for I saw a large table with a fine mirror on it.

Beside the table was an armchair. There sat the strangest lady I have ever seen, or ever

The strangest lady I had ever seen.

shall see. She was dressed in a wedding dress of laces and silks, once all white but now faded almost to yellow. Her shoes were faded too.

There were long-dead bridal flowers in the lady's hair, which was as gray as the dust that covered everything in the room. A handkerchief, some white gloves, a bouquet of flowers, and a prayer book were all heaped on the table, around the mirror.

I immediately realized that the lady was dressed—or at least, had been dressed—for her wedding. Yet, all that had once been white had now lost its luster. And the bride seemed to have withered, just like the flowers in her hair.

"And who are you?" asked the lady at the table.

"Pip, ma'am," I replied. "Mr. Pumblechook brought me to play."

"Come nearer," said the lady. "Let me see you."

It was when I stood before her, avoiding her eyes, that I noticed her watch had stopped at twenty minutes to nine. I also saw that a clock in the room had stopped at the same time.

"Look at me," said Miss Haversham. "You can't be afraid of a woman who has never seen the sun since you were born."

I looked up at her wrinkled face. "Do you know what I touch here?" she said, putting her hand on the left of her chest.

"Your heart, ma'am," I replied.

"Yes," she said. "But it is broken. It broke a long while ago. Now I am tired and want to see some play, to ease the pain. So, boy, play!"

For a moment, I had the desperate idea of pretending to be Uncle Pumblechook's famous carriage. But I daren't.

"What's the matter?" she asked. "Can't you play?"

I replied that I didn't want to get into any trouble, but I found the house too sad to think of playing.

"Call Estella, then," she snapped. "You can do that, can't you?"

I did as I was told and called. The girl who had let me in came out of the darkness, and entered the room.

"Estella," said the lady, "will you play cards with this boy?"

"With *this* boy?" cried Estella. "But he is just a common laboring boy!"

The old lady frowned at her, and she shrugged.

"Oh well, if you insist. Boy, do you know any card games?"

"I know a game called *Beggar My Neighbor*," I replied.

"So beggar him, Estella," said Miss Haversham.

So we sat down to cards. It was then that I began to understand that everything in the room had stopped, like the watch and clock, a long time ago. The wedding dress Miss Haversham was wearing was fit for the grave. And she just sat there, corpse-like, as we played cards.

Estella was very rude to me. She won the first game and announced that I was a stupid, clumsy, ignorant boy. I ignored her taunts, and we started a second game.

Miss Haversham asked me why I hadn't replied to the harsh things Estella said about me.

"I don't like to say," I stammered.

"Whisper them in my ear," said the lady.

I leaned over. "I think she is very proud," I whispered, "and insulting. But she is very pretty. I think I want to go home now."

"What?" asked Miss Haversham. "And never see Estella again?"

Estella won the first game.

"I think I might like to see her again," I replied. "But just now, I would rather go home."

"Finish the game first," said Miss Haversham.

Estella won the second game and threw her cards down in disgust, because I had not made a match of it.

"Come back next Wednesday, boy," said Miss Haversham, "and we'll have some more play."

Estella took me to the garden gate, unlocked it, and let me out without a word. I heard the gate shut behind me as I set off on the journey home.

"What a horrible little girl," I thought, "but how pretty she is."

Chapter 7
Questions and Lies

When I reached home, my sister and Joe were very keen to find out how I had got on with Miss Haversham. So was the bullying old Pumblechook, who had a great curiosity about everything I had seen and heard in the "big house".

"Well, boy," he asked, "how did you get on?"

"Pretty well, sir," I replied.

"Pretty well?" repeated Uncle Pumblechook. "That's no answer. Tell us more."

My sister had already lost patience with me and was about to begin shouting at me, unless I gave her more details.

"Tell me," said Uncle Pumblechook, "what was Miss Haversham like?"

I didn't want to risk getting into trouble by telling them how strange my day had been, and how strange Miss Haversham was. So I invented a new day.

"She was sitting in a black velvet coach in

her bedroom," I replied. "Of course, there weren't any horses attached to the coach. Estella, Miss Haversham's adopted daughter, was there. She served Miss Haversham cake and wine on gold plates, through the coach window. I had to sit on top of the coach to eat my cake."

"Who else was there?" asked Uncle Pumble-chook.

"Four dogs, two small and two large," said I. "They fought for lamb cutlets served on a gold plate."

My sister turned to Uncle Pumblechook and asked if what I had revealed was possible.

"Oh indeed, ma'am," he replied. "Miss Haversham is very strange at times. It sounds just like her."

"Pip," said my sister. "Tell us what you played at."

"We played with flags," I answered. "Estella waved a blue flag and I waved a red one. And Miss Haversham waved one sprinkled all over with little gold stars. Then we all waved some swords and shouted *Hurrah!*"

They both stared at me in disbelief. I think if they had asked any more questions, I would have given myself away. Fortunately, they

I invented a new day.

were so busy discussing my revelations that I escaped from the room with Joe, and went to the forge. There, I admitted the fibs I had told.

"What?" said Joe. "There was no coach, no gold plates, and no dogs?"

"No, Joe," I replied, before going on to explain what an awful day I'd had.

"Miss Haversham was most strange," I began, "and Estella bullied me, and said I was just an ignorant and common laboring boy."

Joe hugged me and told me the lies I had told would be a secret between him and I. "You are not common at all," he said. "You are a most uncommon boy."

"No," I said, "I am common, ignorant, and backward. That's what Estella said."

"You're a proper scholar," replied Joe, "and don't you forget it. A most uncommon scholar."

That night in bed, I wondered how common Estella would find Joe. To my shame, I rather hoped they would never meet.

It had been a big day in my life, and it made for some great changes in me. That was the day I decided I would have to make myself *less* common.

I wanted to learn everything I could from my friend Biddy. She was always so kind to me, and she was very clever. She immediately promised to teach me all she knew. She started me at reading and writing. She spent many hours with me. I was so grateful.

No one was going to call me ignorant and common again.

"You are not common at all."

Chapter 8

A Stranger at the Jolly Sailors Inn

In our village there was an old inn called the Jolly Sailors. That's where Joe escaped from my sister sometimes, to relax. I used to join him on occasions and have a ginger beer.

One night, I went in and found Joe and Mr. Wopsle talking to a man who I had never seen before. He was wearing a broad-brimmed hat. It seemed the man was a stranger to Joe and Mr. Wopsle, too.

"So you're a blacksmith, are you Joe?" the man asked, while looking straight at me in a very strange way.

"Yes I am," said Joe. "Now can I buy you a drink Mr . . .?"

Joe did not know the man's name and the man didn't mention it. He just said that he would buy Joe a drink, instead. The drinks were ordered and while we waited for them, I noticed that the stranger kept staring at me.

The man was a stranger.

Joe introduced Mr. Wopsle to the man as the local parson.

"Oh, you must be the parson of that church out on the marshes," said the stranger. "A lonely place indeed, apart from escaping convicts I expect."

A little later he looked at me again, this time with a half-knowing smile on his lips. Then, while Joe and Mr. Wopsle were talking to each other, the stranger took something from his pocket and started stirring his drink with it.

It was a file. When he had done with it, he wiped it with his handkerchief and returned it to his pocket. It was Joe's file. I knew it instantly. It was the one I had given to the convict.

The thought suddenly hit me—this stranger must know my convict! I sat gazing at him, spellbound. He now settled back in his chair and took very little farther notice of me. But when he got up to go, he leaned across the table, toward me.

"I think I have a bright new shilling somewhere in my pocket," he said, "and if I do, the boy shall have it. I'm sure he has earned it."

He found his shilling and folded it in some crumpled paper, before handing it to me.

Handing the shilling to me

"There. It's yours; a present from a grateful convict," he whispered, before vanishing through the inn door without another word.

When we got home, Joe mentioned the shilling to my sister.

"The man must be a bad 'un," she decided. "Or he wouldn't have given such a large sum of money to the boy. Show it to me."

I took the crumpled paper from my pocket and unwrapped the coin.

As she looked at it, the paper it had been in opened up a little. "What's this?" gasped Mrs. Joe. "If I'm not mistaken, it's two pound notes."

Crumpled they were, but they proved to be two genuine pound notes. Joe thought the man must have wrapped the shilling in the pound notes by mistake. He hurried back to the village to try and find the man, but he was nowhere to be seen. My sister gleefully hid the notes in a teapot.

That night, I had terrible nightmares. I couldn't stop thinking of that stranger, his stares, and the gift of money. I began to think that I had fallen into a conspiracy with some convicts.

I was haunted by that file, too. I dreaded the thought that it might reappear again.

Eventually, I coaxed myself to sleep by thinking about my next visit to Miss Haversham's.

Chapter 9
A Boxing Match

Uncle Pumblechook took me to Miss Haversham's in his coach on the following Wednesday. I rang the bell at the gate, and Estella came and unlocked it. She surprised me by asking whether I still thought she was pretty. I guessed that Miss Haversham had told her what I had said about her on my first visit.

"Yes, I do think you are very pretty," I replied.

"And am I insulting?" she asked.

I didn't know how to answer. I knew she had heard all I had said about her.

"You've lost your tongue now, eh, you little wretch," she snapped. "You were very talkative with Miss Haversham last week, weren't you? You're a gossiping little monster!"

Without another word, she escorted me to Miss Haversham's room and left me. I knocked at the door and entered.

"I want to show you something today," said Miss Haversham.

Taking a stick to help her walk, she took me into a room on the other side of the corridor. It too was totally dark, until she lit a candle. What a sight met my eyes! There was a long table in the middle of the room and on it was what looked like the remains of an uneaten feast. A huge wedding cake stood in the center of the table.

Everything in that room was covered with dust, mold, and cobwebs. I heard mice rattling behind the wooden panels on the walls.

Miss Haversham laid a hand on my shoulder. "This," she said, rattling her stick on the table, "is where I shall be laid when I die . . . in my wedding dress on the wedding feast table. They shall come and look at me here!"

She hit the table with her stick once more. "On this day, long before you were born, this heap of decay—all fresh then—was laid on the table in preparation for my wedding feast. Since then, mice have gnawed at it, while sharper teeth have gnawed at me."

With that, she turned away and led me out of the room. "That's enough for today," she said. "Go and play in the garden for a while, before you go home. But don't forget to come back next week."

The wedding feast table.

I found my way through the dark corridors and out into the garden, where I bumped into a pale young gentleman.

"Who let you wander in the garden?" he asked.

"Miss Haversham," I replied.

"That's alright then," he said. "Now how about a fight? A boxing match, to pass the time of day."

I was so surprised. I assumed it was a normal thing for a gentleman to do. So I said I would. He was now jumping from one foot to the other. Being an obvious gentleman, I assumed he had learned to fight properly.

We set to and I was never more surprised than when I hit him with my first punch. He tumbled to the ground.

"Good punch," he said, politely.

Then he was on his feet straightaway and coming at me again. I knocked him down again. Still he came back for more. I knocked him down one more time, and then he took hold of my hand and raised it, proclaiming me the winner.

"Well fought," said the boy. "Perhaps we'll meet again. My name's Herbert."

With that, he was gone. I set off for the

He took hold of my hand and raised it.

garden gate, only to be met by Estella.

"You said I was pretty," she said. "So do you want a kiss? You may kiss me if you like."

She turned her cheek to me and I kissed it. Then she let me out of the garden and locked the gate behind me.

My mind was racing. Why had Estella asked me to kiss her? And would I be in trouble for fighting with the young gentleman?

When I did return to Miss Haversham's house, there was no mention of the fight and no sign of the boy anywhere. As for Estella, she didn't ask me to kiss her again. But I often overheard Miss Haversham telling her to try and break the hearts of young boys like myself.

"Break their hearts and have no mercy," the old woman would say.

I was not old enough then to realize that she wanted Estella to treat men cruelly, as a sort of revenge on the man who had deserted her on that wedding day, all those years ago.

I must confess, I didn't tell Joe about all the things that happened at Miss Haversham's. But I did take Biddy into my confidence. When I told her about Estella asking for a kiss, she was very concerned. I think Biddy liked me and was jealous that I hadn't asked her for a kiss!

Biddy was jealous.

As for my sister and Uncle Pumblechook, all they wanted to ask me about my visits was whether Miss Haversham had given me anything. They seemed convinced that she had only asked me to visit because she had plans to become my benefactor, and provide me with the means to become something better than a blacksmith's boy.

As for me, I wasn't so keen to be a blacksmith's boy now. I wanted to be *uncommon* enough to win a second kiss from Estella. Somehow, she had managed to make me feel ashamed of my humble home. From a once happy boy, learning my trade with my beloved Joe, I was now a young man all too concerned with not being coarse and common.

I was haunted by the fear that one day, Estella would look through the windows of the forge and see me at my grimy, common work.

Chapter 10
Orlick

Joe employed another young man to help out with the work in the forge. His name was Orlick. He always slouched around, doing as little as possible. He had no liking for me, and I was quite frightened of him. He always said the devil lived in a corner of the forge. Worse still, he said that he knew him well.

"Orlick is a cruel and wicked man," Biddy used to say. "Dare to cross him, and he'll knock you down."

One dark winter night when Joe and I were visiting the village, a terrible thing happened in our house. My sister was violently attacked and left for dead. There was no robbery, and seemingly no motive for the attack.

A broken leg iron was found beside her and to my horror, one end of it had been filed off. I believed it must have been the one that my convict cut off with Joe's file.

Police from London came down to investigate, but they couldn't prove who had done it.

My sister lay unconscious for many days. When she did regain consciousness, she could neither speak nor write. She could tell us nothing about what happened. But in the days ahead, she managed to do a little drawing. It was of a hammer. She drew the same picture, day after day.

We were sure she was referring to the hammer that Orlick used for his daily work.

Yet, whenever Orlick came into the house, she managed a sort of smile and hid her pictures of the hammer. Perhaps she was too terrified to accuse him of the crime.

Nothing could be proved, but Joe was convinced that Orlick was to blame. He told him to leave and find another job. That pleased Biddy, who truly hated Orlick. After that, she came to live with us so that she could care for my sister.

One afternoon I went for a walk with Biddy on the marsh. I talked about Miss Haversham and Estella, and how I wanted to be a gentleman.

"Estella is more beautiful than anyone else I have ever seen," I said. "I admire her terribly. I want to be a gentleman for her."

She drew the same picture, day after day.

"You know best," she said reluctantly. "But aren't you happier as you are?"

"No, I'm not happy," I replied. "I want to improve my life."

"We could have been happy together," she said suddenly.

I knew for sure now, that Biddy was jealous of Estella.

"If only I could make myself fall in love with you," I continued. "Then we could all be happy."

"But you never will," she said sadly.

Just then, Orlick appeared from behind a hedge. I told him that we were having a private talk. He turned away sulkily, but still he followed us for a short distance.

I asked Biddy why she didn't like him. Was it because she thought he had attacked my sister?

"Partly," she said. "But I'm afraid he likes me. He's always looking at me."

That night, I thought hard about Biddy and Estella. They were so different. Biddy was kind, giving, and gentle. Estella was unkind and cruel. So why was she the one I wanted to impress?

I believe I still had at the back of my mind

Orlick appeared from behind a hedge.

the thought that Miss Haversham and Estella, between them, might yet help me to become a gentleman.

Something happened soon after, that made me think that Miss Haversham was interested in helping me. There was a knock on our door one evening. I opened it to find a well-dressed stranger.

"My name is Mr. Jaggers," he announced. "I am a lawyer from London, and I am here on important business. You must be Pip."

"Yes, sir," I replied.

He brushed past me and entered our humble kitchen without further invitation. Joe, Biddy, and my sister all looked up in surprise.

"You must be Joseph Gargery," he said, looking at Joe. "My name is Jaggers, and I have been sent by someone who must remain anonymous. I have been asked to make you an offer. If you are prepared to let Mr. Pip come to London, then I can promise you that he will have great expectations!"

Chapter 11
Great Expectations

Mr. Jaggers was a stern-looking man with thin lips and piercing eyes. I would later discover that he almost never smiled, or laughed. I guessed that he was around fifty years old, though he could have been older. I always heard him coming by the creak of his great black leather boots.

He had a very superior expression on his face as he looked at us all, that night. "Yes," he repeated, "the boy can look forward to great expectations in London if you agree to let him come."

There was silence in the room for a few moments. Then Joe recovered from the shock of the news, and he gave his reply.

"I love the boy dearly and it would break my heart to see him go. But I would do nothing to stand in Pip's way."

Mr. Jaggers continued. "I am instructed by my client to say that the boy will eventually

Mr. Jaggers was a stern-looking man.

inherit some expensive property in London. In the meantime, it is my client's wish that I supply the boy with a regular allowance, and that he should come to London immediately. In short, my client wants Pip to be brought up as a true gentleman."

I could hardly believe what I was hearing. One moment I was talking to Biddy about wanting to be a gentleman, and the next I was told that I was to be brought up a gentleman, and made rich! I was sure it was all to do with Miss Haversham.

"Now you must remember," said Mr. Jaggers, "that the name of your benefactor must remain a secret . . . that is, until the person chooses to reveal it. I can tell you that the person has said that they will reveal it to you personally one day. That may be in many years' time. If you have any suspicion of who that person might be, then you must not breathe a word."

I was in a state of shock and simply nodded in reply.

"Right, boy," said Mr. Jaggers. "First, you are to have some new clothes. I shall leave you twenty pounds to buy these from the local tailor."

Twenty pounds!

Twenty pounds! Rich to me meant twenty pence! Joe watched wide-eyed, as Mr. Jaggers placed twenty pounds onto our table.

"Next Saturday, a week from today, a coach will be provided to carry you to my office in London," Mr. Jaggers continued.

He then turned to Joe again. "The benefactor has told me that he will happily pay you a good sum for compensation."

"What compensation?" asked Joe.

"For the loss of the boy's services in your forge," said Mr. Jaggers.

Joe put his hand on my shoulder. "Pip is free to claim fame and fortune," he said. "I love him as a father loves his dearest son. Better than that, we are the best of friends. Money can't compensate for that."

After Mr. Jaggers had left we all sat in silence, looking at the fire. Joe spoke first. "Pip's a gentleman of fortune then. And God bless him!"

Biddy did her best to try and explain it all to my sister, but it proved impossible. My sister just smiled. Since the attack, she had actually become a far happier person, even though she could not speak, or understand most things.

"A week will soon pass," said Joe, seeing how excited I was.

"Yes, the days will fly," said Biddy, wiping tears from her eyes. "You must show us, when you are all dressed up in your new clothes."

That night when I went up to my bedroom, I was still excited about what was to come. I opened the window and saw that dear Joe was outside, smoking his pipe in the warm summer air.

It came to me then, what I was going to miss when I went away. I suddenly felt I was the loneliest person on earth.

Chapter 12
Preparing to Leave

The next day I walked into the town near our village, to buy new clothes. I went to see Mr. Trubb, the tailor and clothier. When I entered he was gnawing on a leg of chicken.

Mr. Trubb knew me well, but he ignored me completely. He told his young helper to deal with me. "The poor young lad probably wants a cheap handkerchief," I heard him mutter.

"Mr. Trubb," I said, withdrawing the twenty pounds from my pocket. "It may sound like boasting, but I have come into money and property. I have become a man of great expectations. I shall need a fashionable suit of clothes, and some boots and hats, to go to London."

"Bless my soul," cried Mr. Trubb, dropping his chicken and rushing over to me. "May I congratulate you, young sir? And may I show you my finest clothes? May I invite you to take a seat? May I say what an honor it is to serve you? And may I take your measurements?"

"May I take your measurements?"

There was only one more *may I*. He finished measuring me and said, "May I beg to inform you that the suit will be ready in a day or so."

On the way back I bumped into Uncle Pumblechook. He had already heard my news.

"My dear, dear friend," said old Pumblechook, who as far as I knew had never said a kind word to me in his life. "I wish you joy in your good fortune. So well deserved, I say. And may I be so bold as to say that I suspect my good words on your behalf have brought it all about. You are no common boy, as I always used to say to your unfortunate sister!"

I could hardly believe what he was saying to me.

The days quickly passed. On my last night at home, I changed into my new clothes for Joe and Biddy to see. How they laughed when they saw the young gentleman that came downstairs! But there wasn't much laughter in the house that night. We were all thinking of the farewell, the next morning.

I was to leave the village at five o'clock, to meet the London coach. Biddy woke early to prepare my breakfast. And Joe appeared soon after. After breakfast, the moment couldn't be put off any longer.

I was to leave at five o'clock.

"I suppose I must be off," I said sadly. I kissed my sister and Biddy, and then threw my arms around Joe's neck.

I picked up my small case and left the house. Looking back, I saw Joe and Biddy holding each other. I couldn't see their tears, but I knew they were both crying.

Nearer the village the mists were rising, as if to show me the way to my new world. I waited by the village sign, feeling miserable. I was about to run back to the house but then I heard the coach rattling toward me, along the road that led to my new life.

By lunchtime, I had safely arrived in London. I soon found myself seated in Mr. Jaggers's office, which stood in the shadow of the infamous Newgate Prison.

Mr. Jaggers was still in court defending a well-known murderer, so his clerk, a Mr. Wemmick, showed me around. He took great delight in pointing out the Newgate gallows, where many a criminal was hung.

"That's where Mr. Jaggers's present client will probably breathe his last," he said.

He then told me that Mr. Jaggers was famous for defending the most notorious criminals. "He's got as many off free as he's

Pointing out the Newgate gallows

lost to the gallows," he said, "despite their evil crimes."

Mr. Jaggers soon returned to his office. He handed me a list of tradesmen from whom I might buy a gentleman's essentials, and then gave me another twenty pounds to pay for them. "You will find your credit is good in London," he said. "You will not go short of money."

Mr. Jaggers and Wemmick then gave me a quick tour inside Newgate Prison. It was clear that they were both well-known there. I saw many criminals reach through their cell bars to shake both men's hands.

I had a distinct feeling that the two men, while obviously not being criminals, were on very familiar terms with those who were!

Chapter 13
London

Later, Wemmick took me to my new lodgings in a place called Barnard's Inn. I was to stay with a young man called Herbert Pocket. His father, a friend of Mr. Jaggers, was to be my new teacher.

"Mr. Pip?" said Mr. Pocket as Wemmick introduced us.

"Mr. Pocket?" said I.

The moment we looked at each other, we knew we had met before.

"You were the prowling boy I met at Miss Haversham's!" he cried.

"Indeed, sir," said I. "And you were the pale young gentleman. I must apologize for knocking you down so many times."

He laughed. "It was a fair fight and you won it."

"My rooms are not very comfortable," he said politely. "It will be a squeeze, but I hope they will suit. I am happy to share them with you. I shall be delighted to show you around London."

Then he explained why he had been at Miss Haversham's all those years ago.

"Mr. Jaggers was, and probably still is, Miss Haversham's lawyer," he began. "He sent me to Miss Haversham's to be a companion. But it didn't work out. She's such a bitter old woman."

"And you met Estella?" I asked.

"Oh yes," he laughed. "What a haughty creature! She's been brought up by Miss Haversham to wreak revenge on all men."

I wanted to know more about Miss Haversham.

"They say she was the most spoilt child," said Herbert. "Her mother died when she was a baby and her father denied her nothing. She became an heiress. Then she fell deeply in love. The marriage was arranged, and the wedding planned and paid for. The day came, but not the bridegroom. He was never seen again. So the wedding was cancelled at the last minute."

"At exactly twenty minutes to nine," I guessed aloud.

"True," said Herbert. "She stopped all the clocks, the moment she realized he wasn't

We knew we had met before.

going to turn up. She has never seen the light of day since."

That afternoon, Herbert and I walked around London and we got to know each other better. It was clear we were going to be good friends.

Herbert's father was a good teacher, too. He taught me history and languages, while his son taught me to row. Mr. Jaggers gave me another twenty pounds, to buy a rowing boat. Herbert and I used to row on the River Thames together.

Then Mr. Jaggers produced *another* twenty pounds, so I could buy some new furniture for our lodgings.

Herbert was also my guide to table manners. When he saw me load up my knife with peas and put it straight into my mouth, he didn't tell me off as my sister might have. Instead, he politely explained that it was not the custom to put a knife into one's mouth at dinner.

"We reserve the fork for that purpose," he said. "The napkin doesn't go in the glass either, and the spoon is held under the hand, not over it."

My increasing knowledge of how to behave as a gentleman won me a dinner invitation

Herbert was my guide to table manners.

from Mr. Jaggers. Wemmick, Mr. Jaggers's clerk, was also there. As was a dull, pompous fellow called Bentley Drummle—another rower I had seen on the Thames. Bentley Drummle's father was very rich, and well-known in London.

Molly, Mr. Jaggers's housekeeper, was to serve us. Molly was about forty years old and looked as though she had been beautiful once.

As the meal proceeded we began talking about rowing, and how strong wrists were needed to be good at it.

Mr. Jaggers, never one to miss introducing one of his favorite topics into the conversation, observed that he had defended many a strangler in court. "Some of them had very strong wrists," he said.

Just then, Molly came in with coffee for us. Once she had put down the coffee cups, Mr. Jaggers caught hold of her hands.

"See here," he chuckled, as if he was telling a private joke. "Gentlemen, if you want to talk of strong wrists, I'll show you a good pair. Go on Molly, show 'em your wrists."

She reluctantly displayed her hands and wrists for us.

"See," said Mr. Jaggers. "Very few men have

wrists as strong as Molly's. It's remarkable the grip she has!"

Then he let her go. Wemmick winked mischievously at me, as though he knew why Mr. Jaggers had shown Molly's wrists. I couldn't understand what they found so amusing.

I had been so busy staring at Molly's wrists that I hadn't really looked closely at her face. When I did, I had the strangest sensation that I had seen her eyes before . . . and if not Molly's eyes, then I'd met someone with eyes very much like hers . . .

Chapter 14
Convicts on the Coach

I had sent news of my address to Joe and Biddy, and a few days later I received a letter.

My Dear Mr. Pip,
Joe has asked me to write to let you know that he is going to London with Mr. Wopsle. He plans to come to your rooms at nine o'clock on Tuesday morning.
Your poor sister is much the same as when you left. We talk of you every night and wonder what you are doing.
Your ever affectionate servant,
Biddy.

Herbert and I were both at home when Joe arrived. He was looking well. I hung up his hat and introduced him to Herbert.

It was clear that the humble blacksmith felt ill at ease in the company of a gentleman and a would-be gentleman. His eyes were soon rolling at seeing the comfortable and

Joe felt ill at ease.

well-decorated rooms; not to mention the fancy flower pattern on the dressing gown I had bought.

"Do you take tea or coffee?" Herbert asked.

"Thankee, sir," he replied. "I'll take whichever is most agreeable to you."

"It's tea then," said Herbert, pouring it out.

Joe sipped at his tea, looking unhappy.

"Have you seen much of London yet?" asked Herbert.

"A little sir; we visited the Blacking Warehouse," he replied. "That were interesting. Very architectooralooral."

Poor Joe couldn't get his tongue around the word *architectural.* That embarrassed him. He was so uncomfortable that, at one point, he even called me *sir.*

He stayed a couple of hours and finally passed on a message from Miss Haversham. It was that Estella would be very glad to see me.

At last, Joe got up. "I'm sorry I have to go now and meet Mr. Wopsle, and catch the coach home."

Then he gave me a hug. "Bless you, dear old Pip. But your smart new world is not for me; I yearn to be back in the forge with my hammer and anvil."

By his visit, Joe had demonstrated to me yet again what a kind and caring man he was.

The mention of Estella had upset me. I decided that I must travel down to see her the very next day. I booked a place on a coach.

It was the habit in those days for convicts to be transported under guard in a coach. My coach carried two escaped convicts, being returned to the prison hulks near my old home.

I was badly shaken when, as I was boarding the coach, I saw that one of them was the very same stranger I had seen in the Jolly Sailors Inn. He was the man who stirred his drink with Joe's file, before giving me a shilling wrapped up in two pound notes.

I quickly hid my head and took my seat. Fortunately, the convicts were sitting on the outside of the coach, behind me. It was terrifying to know that they were so close.

A little way into the journey, they began talking about none other than myself! They were whispering about a prisoner who had escaped at Christmas, some years before. It must have been *my* convict. It seemed that after he had been returned to the hulk, he asked a favor of anyone who was planning to escape.

"When he heard that I was going to escape," said the one whose face I knew, "he came to me and asked me to hunt down a little boy who had helped him on the marsh. He gave me two pound notes to give to him. And to make sure the boy knew where it had come from, he gave me a small file to show him."

"Did you find the boy?" asked the second man.

"Yes, at an inn close to the boy's home. I showed him the file first. The poor boy's face went white. Then I gave him the money."

"You're an idiot," said the second man. "I would have taken the money for myself."

"No," said the other. "It was a matter of honor. The other convict felt the boy had saved his life with the food and drink he brought him."

"Where's that convict now?" asked the other man.

"He was given a life sentence for escaping, and transported to Australia," he answered. "And there, by law, he must remain for the rest of his life."

I quickly hid my head.

Chapter 15

I See Estella Again

I was glad to get off that coach without the convicts recognizing me. I hurried off to Miss Haversham's. At the locked gate, I was astonished to see a familiar face.

"Orlick!" I cried.

"Yes, things have changed around here," he said. "I'm now Miss Haversham's gatekeeper and porter."

I had no wish to talk with Orlick and asked him to show me in. I found Miss Haversham in her dressing room with Estella.

"Do you find Estella much changed, Pip?" asked Miss Haversham.

"She is more beautiful than I ever remembered her," I said, feeling like a very common blackmith's boy once again.

"Has he changed much?" Miss Haversham asked Estella.

"Very much," she replied. "Much less common and coarse."

"Has he changed much?"

Miss Haversham sent us out to walk in the gardens.

"I believe," said Estella, "that since you came into money you have changed your companions."

"Naturally," I replied.

"And very necessarily," she added. "What was fit company for you once, would be quite unfit company for you now."

It was those words that made me decide not to visit Joe and Biddy later that day, even if I did feel very ashamed of myself. But as we talked, I knew things hadn't changed between us.

At one point Estella said, "However much you adore me, you must always remember that I have no heart. There is no softness or sympathy there."

I was silent after that. How I loved her now! Yet I clearly saw that however much love I showed her, she never made me happy.

As we walked back, I mentioned that Orlick was not to be trusted. "He'll rob Miss Haversham as easily as he could smile at her," I warned.

Back in London, I felt so guilty about not visiting Joe and Biddy that I sent them a large barrel of oysters to enjoy.

The next day I received a note from Estella.

Dear Mr. Pip,
I am coming to London tomorrow by the
midday coach. Please meet me.
Yours,
Estella.

Estella duly arrived, but she hadn't really
come to see me. All she wanted was for me to
escort her to Richmond, some five miles off,
to see a great lady.

How I loved her now!

"You must take me to her immediately," she snapped. "The lady is to introduce me to London society. I may have time to see you very occasionally. But I expect I will be very busy with some very wealthy families."

So, after taking her to Richmond, we parted again. In the days ahead, I never lost the chance to haunt the streets of Richmond, hoping to see her. If I had met her, I had no idea what excuse I would have given for being there.

Soon after Estella's arrival, I received a letter from Biddy. My sister had died.

I immediately wrote to Joe, saying I would be coming to the funeral.

Chapter 16
My Sister's Funeral

The funeral was a sad affair. Joe was heart-broken and kept saying, "She were a fine figure of a woman."

Old Pumblechook drank all the sherry at the funeral dinner. And Mr. Hubble, the wheel maker, drank all the port. Uncle Pumblechook spent the rest of the funeral telling everyone who cared to listen that he was the founder of my fortune.

That evening, I walked with Biddy toward the marsh. I could see how much she liked me still. Now that my sister was dead, she would leave Joe to take up a teaching job at a new school nearby. Biddy promised that she would return every day to make sure Joe was alright.

"Joe never complains of anything," she said. "He has worked his way through life with a strong hand, a quiet tongue, and a gentle heart."

I also promised her that I would come to see both of them as often as I could.

"Are you quite sure you will come?" she asked.

"What do you mean?" I replied angrily. "How could you think I wouldn't?"

"We'll see, won't we," she answered.

That made me very angry. Soon after we returned home, I went to my little bedroom for the night. I fell asleep thinking how unfair Biddy had been in suggesting I might not come to see them regularly.

In the morning, Joe and Biddy said goodbye to me.

"Dear Joe, I shall be down again soon and often," I said.

"It'll never be too soon or too often," replied Joe.

But I didn't keep my word. There was so much to do in London. I was always making excuses for not taking the coach home. Herbert and I were out most nights, enjoying ourselves, both spending more than we ought.

On my twenty-first birthday, I went to Mr. Jaggers and asked whether he could say when my benefactor might appear. He replied that it was a question he could not answer yet.

Then, as I had become very short of money,

I was very angry.

I asked whether I was to receive anything on my birthday.

Mr. Jaggers looked at me severely. "You are in debt, aren't you?" he said. "You have not looked after your financial affairs very well. But you have one more chance."

He handed me a wad of pound notes, tied up with pink ribbon. "Your benefactor has given you five hundred pounds for your birthday. On top of that, you are to receive five hundred pounds each year to live on, and no more. You must learn to manage your money until you come into your great expectations, later."

I promised him I'd try harder. But my good intentions didn't last long. No sooner was I out of Mr. Jaggers's office, than I bumped into Wemmick.

"Wemmick," I said, "Herbert and I have been good friends for some time now, but he is very short of money. I would like to help him . . . find him a business opportunity. I could invest some of my money in him now, and perhaps, let him have more later. But I don't want him to have any idea who has helped him."

Wemmick promised, and a few days later he found a man looking for both investment and a

MR. JAGGERS
Attorney

"I would like to help him."

partner. He was a young shipping merchant by the name of Clarriker. I was happy to invest five hundred pounds in my friend Herbert — my whole year's allowance.

Wemmick quietly informed Herbert that he had found a man wanting a business partner. It gave me great joy when Herbert came home that evening and told me the news that he had been taken on in a business.

My own fortunes with Estella were going from bad to worse. I visited her regularly and on one of my visits to her, she had repeated that she could never fall in love with me. "And if you can't see that, you're blind," were her exact words.

A few days later, I discovered that she had been seen at a ball, dancing with the wealthy rower I had met at Mr. Jaggers's dinner, Bentley Drummle.

"Why do you give him the time of day?" I protested when I saw her next. "You know how much that hurts me."

"It's not worth discussing," she said. "I dance with many different men."

"Yes," I replied, getting angrier. "And you give them all fine looks and smiles, such as you never give me!"

"Do you want me to deceive and entrap you, like I do them?" she asked.

"Do you deceive and entrap them?" I asked.

"Yes, many of them," she said. "All of them, in fact, except you."

Estella always knew how to keep me hanging on to her.

Chapter 17

A Ghost from the Past

The years passed very quickly. Before I knew it, I was celebrating my twenty-third birthday—an occasion marked by an unexpected visitor.

Herbert was abroad on business with Mr. Clarriker. It was a wretched day with a violent storm sweeping across London. The streets were covered in puddles and mud. I settled down in front of the fire at my lodgings.

I heard the chimes of St. Paul's ring out nine o'clock. The next moment, I heard footsteps coming up the stairs.

I opened my door and looked down. In the dim light of my lamp, I saw a man. He was about sixty years old, and by the way he was dressed, could have been a seaman. He was very muscular, and browned and hardened by exposure to the weather.

"What's your business, sir?" I asked.

"You are my business, Mr. Pip," he said.

"What's your business, sir?"

"You know my name, sir," I replied with surprise.

"Aye, that I do," he said, holding out both his hands towards me.

"What do you want?" I asked, becoming very nervous.

"It's disappointing for a man who has traveled so far not to be recognized," he said. "But you're not to blame for that. I'll explain in half a minute."

Without an invitation, he walked into my rooms and sat himself down by the fire. "There's no one about, is there?" he asked suspiciously.

"Why should a stranger coming into my home at this time of night ask that question?" I asked.

"You're a game one, aren't you," he replied. "I'm glad you've grown up a game one. I thought you would."

That was the moment! It's true that I didn't recognize him at first. But I knew who he was. I couldn't be surer!

The wind and rain howled outside, blowing away the years. It was more than fifteen years since I had seen him.

There was no need for him to take a

familiar file out of his pocket; no need to hug himself with both arms to keep warm. I needed no clues. He was my convict!

Now he held his hands out again. I found myself giving mine to him. He pressed them to his lips.

"You acted nobly," he said. "Noble Pip! I've never forgot it."

I panicked and pushed him away. "Have you repented your crimes?" I muttered, too much in shock to know what to say.

"I've paid for 'em," he replied.

"I'm glad to hear it," I said, "but you must understand . . ."

"What must I understand?" he asked.

"Things have changed so much since we met," I sighed. "And I thank you for coming to say you were grateful for what I did. But it's been a long time, and we have both changed and gone our different ways."

It was then that I saw his eyes were full of tears. Up until that moment, I had wished him gone. But now I softened. "I'm sorry if I spoke harshly to you," I said. "I wish you well, I really do."

"I understand," he said. "I was in Australia a long time, thinking about you."

I saw his eyes were full of tears.

"I heard you were in Australia," I said, recalling the conversation between the two convicts I had overheard in the coach. I asked him if he remembered giving some money to a convict to hand over to me.

"Oh, yes, I did," he answered, with a smile. "That was before they put me on a boat and sailed me all the way to Australia. And Australia wasn't all bad. After a few years they allowed me to start a small farm. I turned that into a bigger farm. I became a sheep farmer and stock breeder. I did wonderfully well. In fact, I became very rich."

"Well, we have something in common," I said. "We both seem to have come into fortunes."

He smiled. "May I be so bold as to ask where your fortune came from?"

"I have been chosen to inherit some property," I said. "There's money to go with it. I've been told I have great expectations."

"Might I make a guess," he said, "and suggest the annual sum you are receiving? Would it be, say, five hundred pounds?"

My heart started beating like a hammer.

"And would the name of your guardian be a lawyer, whose name begins with a *J?*" he

105

continued. "And would he be a Mr. Jaggers, who has a clerk called Wemmick?"

I seemed to be suffocating. I couldn't breathe properly.

"Yes, Pip, dear boy," he said. "It was me who made a gentleman of you."

At last, I knew for certain who my benefactor was. It wasn't Miss Haversham after all. It was a criminal lucky not to have ended his life on the gallows already.

I was, suddenly, no longer a gentleman in the making. I could see disgrace on the horizon if the true identity of my benefactor were to become known.

Chapter 18
The Convict's Story

"Yes, my boy," said the man, "It was me that done it! I swore that whenever I earned a pound, I'd send it to you in thanks. Without that food and drink, I'd have died on that marsh. And when I got rich, I told myself that you should be rich too. I lived rough, so you could live smooth. I worked hard, so you wouldn't have to."

He sat down by the fire. "Do I tell you all this to make you feel obliged to me?" he continued. "Oh no, my boy. I did it in thanks, and to make you a gentleman. Lookee here, Pip, I'm your second father."

I just didn't know what to do. In a strange way, I dreaded him being so close to me.

"Did you ever think that I was your benefactor?" he asked.

"Never! Never!" I said.

"So you see," he said, "it was me single-handed who did it."

"I'm your second father."

"Are you sure?" I asked at last. "Are you sure there was no one else involved?"

"No!" he cried. "Who else should there be?"

He then asked whether he could sleep the night in my rooms. I could not turn him away. He looked exhausted and half-asleep already. I told him that I shared the rooms with Herbert, and that he was away. "He won't be back until tomorrow," I said.

"Is he to be trusted?" he asked, suddenly looking all around him rather suspiciously.

"Yes," I replied. "But why should that worry you?"

"Lookee here, dear boy," he said. "It's dangerous. Much caution is needed."

"How do you mean, caution?" I asked.

"Because it's death to me," he said. "The sentence I received for escaping was to be sent to Australia for life. Yes, I made my fortune there. But life still means life. If anyone finds me here, I would be hanged. That's a certainty."

I was left speechless again. I ran across to close the window shutters and lock the doors. I showed him the room where he was to sleep. He lay on the bed and closed his eyes immediately.

At last, I had time to think about the consequences of my benefactor's arrival.

The worst thing, as far as I was concerned, was that for so long I had lived my life thinking that Miss Haversham was my benefactor, and wanted to groom me as a gentleman to marry Estella.

Now my every thought was of a constable coming through my door and taking off the convict to be hung outside Newgate Prison. And me with him, perhaps.

Later, I crept into the bedroom where he was sleeping. There was a pistol lying on his pillow.

There was no way I could hide this man in my rooms. He would soon be discovered. I had a cleaning lady who came in three times a week. She had very weak eyesight and I put that down to the fact that she spent too much time looking through keyholes. So he wouldn't be safe with her about.

For the time being, I decided to tell anyone who visited me that a long-lost uncle had arrived to stay.

When my convict got up, he looked even more frightening that the night before.

"I'm going to pretend you're my uncle," I said.

"That's it, dear boy! Call me uncle," he said.

I asked him what his real name was.

"For now, I go under the name of Mr. Provis," he answered, "but I can trust you with my real name. It's Abel Magwitch."

"I shall call you Uncle Provis then, when anyone is around," I said. "But tell me more about yourself. What were you brought up to be?"

"A rogue, my boy. A rogue."

"Are you known in London?" I asked.

I ran across to close the window.

"I mostly worked outside of London," he said, "but I have appeared in court in London often enough. Mr. Jaggers, with Wemmick's help, defended me in court. That's how I know 'em. They're the best men in town for defending us rogues.

"I don't know where I was born, nor who my father or mother was. I've no idea who called me Abel Magwitch. But that's the name I grew up with. My first memory is of stealing carrots from a field to save myself from starving. I was put in the stocks and whipped for that.

"Then I became a soldier, but soon deserted. I was in and out of jail after that. One day, I met a gentleman. He'd been to a good school and spoke well. He used me to do his thieving for him. He used me to crack people's skulls if they didn't give him what he wanted. And when we was caught, the judge let him off because he was a gentleman.

"Me? He sent me to jail for ten years. It was Mr. Jaggers, with Wemmick's help, who defended me. I would have got a life sentence without Mr. Jaggers's help. Mind you, I gave myself a life sentence when I escaped from the convict hulk."

Magwitch turned to look at me closely.

"My first memory is of stealing carrots."

"They call me a hard man," he said, "yet whatever I've done, whatever crimes I have committed in the past, they're all worked and paid for now. Old Magwitch deserves a little freedom and sympathy now."

Chapter 19
Plotting and Planning

After breakfast, Magwitch announced that he had plans for me. "Lookee here," he said, "a gentleman needs a horse and a carriage. I shall buy them for you. My young gentleman mustn't be seen to be short of any of life's necessities."

"We've got more important things to think about," I sighed. "First, we must buy you some better clothes. Then we must think about hiding you. Are you known by many people in London?"

He thought before answering. "There's Jaggers and Wemmick and you, and no doubt a few others, of a more criminal nature. But I ain't going to advertize my arrival in the newspapers, am I."

I decided to go and buy him some clothes. I returned later and he tried them on. But there was something about the man. The better dressed he was, the more he looked like the slouching convict I had first met on the marshes!

That same morning, Herbert arrived home. He was quite shaken to be met by a man who, on hearing him enter, produced a shining jack-knife to defend himself.

I hurriedly jumped between them. "Herbert," I said. "Something very strange has happened. This is a visitor of mine."

"And this visitor will strike you dead," announced Magwitch, "if you turn me in."

I calmed them both down and then explained to Herbert about Magwitch and I.

"Well," said Herbert at last, "I'm not sure I know what to do next. I am too stunned!"

Later that day, when Magwitch was sleeping, Herbert came up with an idea.

"It seems to me," he said, "that the first thing to do is to get him out of the country. He can't stay in London, unless you want to see him hanged."

I replied that I didn't want to see poor Magwitch hanged on my account.

"Right," said Herbert, "we'll think this one through. Now it's clear that it will soon be known that Magwitch has left Australia. So there'll be a watch put out on all the ports

I hurriedly jumped between them.

in England. They'll guess that he must be making for England. So if we can get him out of England quickly we can see it through, old boy."

I felt more relaxed now that I had my good friend Herbert to share the responsibility of Magwitch. It was Herbert's job with the shipping merchant Clarriker that gave us the means to get Magwitch out of the country. There were boats that left London for Europe every day of the week.

"Now," said Herbert, "if we could smuggle Magwitch aboard one of those, our problems would be over. My work has given me connections in Europe. I could find him a ship to a port in Europe."

Long into the night, we discussed possibilities and worked out a plan. It was too dangerous to put Magwitch aboard a ship while it was still in the Port of London. The river police kept a careful watch on all boats.

What we wanted was a foreign ship that regularly sailed for Europe. Then we needed to find a spot where the outward-bound ship would still be going relatively slowly. We could then row out to meet it, and safely pull alongside the vessel.

Herbert said that a foreign captain could easily be bribed to take an extra passenger. He said he would find out more about the ships, while I set about finding a safe place to hide Magwitch.

Herbert studied ship's timetables and also, the times of high and low tides. Meanwhile, I discovered the Ship Inn, a remote hostelry on the Thames. I paid for a room that overlooked the river.

Magwitch seemed quite happy with both our plan and his new home. We smuggled him downriver that very night and got him settled in. I told him that to maintain secrecy I wouldn't be able to come down and see him very often.

"I know I have no choice really," he admitted to me. "So I'd rather see my gentleman occasionally than not at all. And it would be not at all if they caught and hung me. Besides, I can always return to England when all the hue and cry has calmed down, and they've all forgotten about me."

Soon Herbert had identified a German ship called the *Hamburg* that came in and out of London every three days. It was ideal. He could sail on the *Hamburg* to a port in

Germany, and take another ship from there to Australia. We began regular daily expeditions down the Thames in my rowing boat.

By rowing the same route each day, the patrolling river police got used to seeing us, and ignored us. We soon identified a place a few miles downriver from the Ship Inn, where we could intercept the German ship.

Amid all this plotting and planning, I received an urgent message from Miss Haversham, asking me to go and see her.

Smuggling Magwitch downriver

Chapter 20
Guesses and Confessions

Before I could go down to see Miss Haversham, I had to visit Mr. Jaggers to talk about my finances. As I sat outside his office and waited to see him, Wemmick whispered in my ear that he'd heard something of interest on the criminal grapevine.

Apparently, police constables were already searching London for a certain escaped convict from Australia! I did not know what to say in reply. It seemed Wemmick knew everything . . .

Mr. Jaggers, of course, also knew all about the arrival of Magwitch in London. Not that he would admit to it. Mr. Jaggers never admitted anything.

"If the man is in London," said Jaggers, "then it's nothing to do with me. And if it's money you need, I'm afraid you will have to learn to live on your own efforts for the time being. The sources have temporarily dried up."

I wondered desperately what I would do for money—and what I would do if Magwitch was caught.

Before I left, Mr. Jaggers asked me to dinner. Perhaps he felt sorry for me. That evening I finally realized why, on our first dinner, I had been puzzled by the eyes of Molly, his housekeeper.

Now, as she entered the dining room, I saw that her eyes were identical to Estella's eyes! And her face was so similar to Estella's. *Could Molly be Estella's mother?*

As Wemmick escorted me to the door after dinner, I asked him some questions.

"When did Molly become Mr. Jaggers's housekeeper?" I asked.

"Oh, many years ago," he replied. "Twenty years or so."

"What do you know about her past?" I went on.

"She was a rogue," he replied. "She was married once, then she went off with another man. They fought tooth and nail all the time. One day, he was found dead. She was charged with his murder but she was found not guilty, mainly due to the clever defense made in court by her lawyer."

Could Molly be Estella's mother?

"I assume her lawyer was Mr. Jaggers?" I said, with a smile.

"Ah, yes," said Wemmick.

I now remembered Mr. Jaggers mysteriously showing us Molly's powerful wrists, during my first dinner.

"Tell the truth, Wemmick," I said. "She strangled her husband with those powerful wrists, didn't she?"

"She might have done," winked Wemmick, who rather like his master, didn't like admitting anything. "Mr. Jaggers bought her a special dress with very long sleeves to wear in court. The jury never saw the strength of her wrists. If they had, they might have believed she was guilty of murder. He employed her as a housekeeper immediately after the case.

"Did Molly have a child?" I asked. I was just guessing now, but I had a theory.

"Yes, I remember she did have a small child by her husband," nodded Wemmick. "But I never saw the child after the trial. She gave it away, I think, because she couldn't look after it. But to whom she gave it, I don't know. The child would have been about three years old at the time."

"Was the child a girl?" I asked.

"Yes," said Wemmick.

Now I was more curious than ever!

***

The next day I traveled down to Miss Haversham's. There was a look of utter loneliness on the old lady's face when we met again, in the room where the wedding feast lay.

"The reason I asked you to call was to show you that I am not all stone," she said. "I do have a heart. And I hope one day you will be able to forgive me."

"Oh Miss Haversham, I forgive you already," I said. "We have all made mistakes in life. And my life has been full of them."

To my surprise, for the first time, I saw tears in her eyes. "I was treated cruelly when the man I was to marry deserted me," she began. "And ever since, I have used Estella to take my revenge on other men—even you, dear Pip. But, by my actions, I stole away her heart and put it on ice. It was a terrible thing to do."

"Whose child was Estella?" I asked, taking the chance to ask a question I desperately wanted the answer to.

"I don't know," she said.

"I forgive you already."

"You don't know?" I replied, quite surprised.

"No," she said. "I asked Mr. Jaggers to find me an orphan child to love. Then one night he turned up with a beautiful young girl. I called her Estella and adopted her, but I never knew where she came from. Mr. Jaggers said he was not free to reveal her true identity."

I was now certain that Molly was Estella's true mother!

Later, I left Miss Haversham, still dressed in her tattered and yellowing wedding dress. As I walked out of the house, I looked up to the window of her room.

I heard a shriek. Something had happened! The window, behind which she had hidden for so many years, burst open. For a moment, I saw the old lady silhouetted against a whirl of flame. She was on fire!

I flew back into the house and raced up to Miss Haversham's room. Sparks from a candle must have caught her tinder-dry wedding dress. I pulled a curtain from the window, and threw it over her. She was still screaming when I finally extinguished the blaze.

A surgeon was called and he told me to clear the wedding table. He wanted Miss

Haversham to be laid on the table, to be examined. It was as if her wish was to come true. All those years ago, she had told me that she wanted to die and be laid out on the wedding table for all to see.

I took hold of one corner of the table cloth and pulled it violently. The remains of that wedding feast crashed to the floor, and Miss Haversham took its place.

While the surgeon did his best, I held

She was on fire!

Miss Haversham's hand. For a long time, she hovered between life and death. At last she turned to me. "Please forgive me," she said very faintly.

She died soon after.

Chapter 21
Estella's Father

When I returned to London I was met by Herbert, who had surprising news.

"I talked with Magwitch last night and he told me a lot more about himself," said my friend, as we walked back to our lodgings. "Do you know, he thinks he may have a daughter who is still alive."

"Tell me more," I said.

Herbert repeated to me exactly what Magwitch had told him. Apparently he had once been married, more than twenty years earlier. The woman had been a villain in her own right, he said. They had a child but while it was still a baby, she had left Magwitch and taken the babe.

"He hasn't seen the child since," added Herbert. "He doesn't blame the woman. He said that he had given her as rough a time as she had given him."

I asked Herbert if Magwitch had said anything about his former wife being charged with murdering another man.

"Indeed, he did," replied Herbert. "He'd heard that soon after his wife left him, she had been charged with murdering a man. But he hadn't bothered to find out what had happened to her, or the baby. In any case, he would have been in Australia after that."

My puzzle was complete, and Mr. Jaggers's bewildering role in the whole mystery unraveled. Mr. Jaggers, as I well knew, never liked to admit anything. Yet he knew of Molly's secret past all along—that Estella was Molly's child, and that Magwitch was both the father of the child and my benefactor.

"I can now tell you something, dear Herbert," I said. "I now know that the man we have in hiding down the river is Estella's father. And that her mother is Molly, Mr. Jaggers's housemaid!"

Herbert was astonished when I told him all that I had found out.

That night Herbert set off for France on business. Two days later I found a note on my doormat. It had been delivered by hand. It said:

Meet me by the old limekiln on the marsh tomorrow night, at midnight. A man's life is at risk. You can help save him. And if you want

Herbert had surprising news.

some additional information about your "Uncle Provis" that may be of value, I have it for you. You must come!

The note was unsigned and I didn't recognize the writing. The last thing I wanted was to venture out on that marsh in the middle of the night. But I felt I had no choice if a man's life was at risk . . . and something was known about my "Uncle Provis", who of course, was Magwitch.

I caught the afternoon coach the next day. As the coach approached my village, I felt in my pocket and realized that I had left the note behind. I thought it didn't really matter, as I knew the time and place of the meeting.

I set out across the marshes. The limekiln was nowhere near my old home. It stood in the loneliest part of the marsh. The kiln was used to make lime, a powder used to kill insects in the soil. It was also well known among some of Mr. Jaggers more murderous clients, as a chemical that would quickly destroy flesh and bone . . .

It was a very dark night and rain was pouring down. As I drew close to the limekiln, my legs began to shake with fear. There wasn't a sign of anyone about but I saw a candle flickering on a table, through the open door of the kiln.

I walked over to the table and before I knew it, the door had crashed shut behind me. "Got you!" a voice screamed out. "Got you, you miserable creature!"

I turned to find myself facing Orlick. He had a musket, which was aimed at my head.

"I have a bone to pick with you," he snarled.

"Let me go!" I shouted.

"Ah," he said, "I'll let you go in good time. I'll let you go to the moon or the stars. All in good time."

"What do you want, Orlick?" I asked. "Why have you lured me here?"

"For revenge," he answered, waving the musket at me.

"Revenge for what?" I asked, still shaking badly.

"You may well shake," he snorted. "You cost me that place at Miss Haversham's. You told her that I was a bit of no good! I lost that job because of you. And your father sacked me, too."

"You brought those things on yourself," I protested.

My legs began to shake with fear.

"Oh, I might have given reason for your father to sack me," he continued. "Yet I never hurt your sister. Yes, I hit her hard with the edge of an old leg iron I found on the marsh. Funny that; it seemed to have been cut with a file! I always did wonder why you were down on the marsh on that long-ago Christmas morning. You didn't see me, but I saw you.

"So it was the leg iron that hurt your sister, not me. And you were to blame, because I think you helped that escaped convict. Anyway; you and your family always treated me like dirt. Joe always praised you and kept you as his favorite. He gave me nothing. And I might have married Biddy, but for you. You turned her against me!"

"You were just a liar and a cheat," I said, fighting back at last. "And you never did a day's work in your life! As for Biddy, she always distrusted and hated you."

"Argh! Never mind!" he cried, in a mad sort of way. "You are going to pay for it all. I'm going to have your life. Old Orlick's had enough of you. He's going to kill you and bury you in quicklime. They'll be nothing left of you in next to no time."

Chapter 22
My Last Thoughts

Desperate last thoughts flew through my mind. I had left no note where I was going. And, for sure, I would never be seen again. Abel Magwitch would think I had deserted him. Herbert would be puzzled for the rest of his life. Joe and Biddy would never know how much I loved them, and now regretted forgetting them.

"I'll tell you something before you go," he said. "Since I left Miss Haversham's, I've teamed up with some new employers. They employ me to skulk around London's darkest corners, looking for people and places to rob.

"Now I was down at the Ship Inn recently, and who should I see but your good self and a certain Uncle Provis. Now there's a funny name, ain't it? Yet that's the name I heard you call him as you left the inn. But I recognized the man. I saw him on the marsh when he was recaptured, when you were just a little seven-year-old.

"I knew that man was really old Abel Magwitch. What's more, I kept watch on your lodgings, and listened at the door on many a night. So you're thinking of getting him away to Europe, are you? I doubt it, old Pip. Magwitch will hang now for sure, especially when I tell the river police where to find him. They'll pay me handsomely for the news, too."

I would never be seen again.

He took another step forward and I shrank away from him. "Now, it's time to say good-bye," he said, a cruel smile twisting on his lips.

I waited for the shot, but it never came. Instead, he dropped the gun and picked up a huge hammer that was used to crush lime.

I can hardly remember clearly what happened next. But as Orlick raised the hammer, ready to strike, the door suddenly burst open and a figure appeared.

That's when I fainted.

***

When I awoke, it was still night. I found that I was in a coach on the way back to London. My dearest friend Herbert was sitting beside me. He had returned to London and found the note that I had accidentally left behind. He'd hired an express coach to bring him to the marshes.

Of course, Herbert had no idea where the limekiln was. But a local lad showed him the way. He had been outside the kiln and had heard a great deal of the conversation. When he peeked through a crack in the door and saw Orlick raise the hammer, he burst in to

Orlick raised the hammer, ready to strike.

save me.

"I hit him far harder than I ever hit you when we first met at Miss Haversham's," laughed Herbert. "He's probably still unconscious. I tied him up and left him there."

"What!" I cried. "Didn't you call the police to take him?"

"And have him reveal all about Magwitch?" said Herbert. "No, we simply must get Magwitch away before Orlick escapes, and reveals what he knows. The *Hamburg* sails on the high tide tomorrow morning. It's a matter of Magwitch's life or death, my dear boy!"

When we arrived in London in the early hours of the next morning, Herbert went to see Wemmick, who arranged to alert Magwitch that he must be ready to leave immediately. Magwitch was to wait on the riverside for our arrival.

Herbert and I hurried to the river to launch our boat. It was only a two man rowing boat but it was speedy enough. We set off down the river as fast as we could, passing London Bridge and the Tower of London under cover of darkness.

We raced past the docks where we saw the *Hamburg,* an old paddle steamer, loading up.

It was a few hours until high tide, and the ship wouldn't leave before then.

We reached the Ship Inn soon after and saw that Magwitch was ready for us. With his dark cloak, he looked every inch a Thames boatman.

"Dear boy," he said, jumping aboard. "I'm ready for this great adventure, and I thankee for it."

Old Abel Magwitch seemed to be the only one who wasn't terrified of what might lie ahead.

"If you know what it's like to sit here along with my dear gentlemen, after spending so many days waiting," he chuckled, "you'd know how happy I am. It's wonderful to be free and taking a pleasure trip down the River Thames with two of my best friends."

"If all goes well," I said, "in a few hours you should be even freer."

"And I hope so, my boy!" he said. "The sooner it happens, the sooner I'll be able to sail back to Australia and welcome my gentleman to my new country."

He lit his pipe and settled back in his seat.

We raced past the docks.

Chapter 23
The Hamburg

It was cold on the river but ahead in the east, I could just make out the first color of the new day. The tide was going out strongly, and the current flowed faster and faster downriver.

By the time the sun had stepped over the horizon, we were nearing our destination. The next bend in the river was to be our waiting point, on the north shore. We reached it just as the tide turned.

The place was just where the Thames changed from a river into an estuary. Looking across to the southern shore in the distance, I could see the marshes of my childhood. I couldn't see the limekiln, but I knew in which direction it lay. I thought of Orlick tied up inside, not more than three miles from where we stood. The thought of him sent shivers down my spine.

The tidal water that had carried us down-river, now turned and set about returning to

London where it would, at high tide, help float the *Hamburg* down to us. We hid ourselves and the boat among a bed of reeds, to await its arrival. Nobody spoke. Even Magwitch sensed the tension now.

It was past midday when Herbert suddenly stood up and looked upriver. "Smoke!" he cried. "Let's hope it's the *Hamburg*."

We could all see the smoke of a steamer. A few minutes later we saw the ship, its paddles circling, drawing closer to us.

"It's definitely the *Hamburg*," I said. "Let's go."

We clambered back into the boat. Then Herbert and I pulled hard at the oars, and moved out into the estuary, heading to a point where we would cross the ship's path.

We got there in good time, with the *Hamburg* still some way off.

"Look!" cried Herbert. "Another boat's coming."

For a moment I couldn't see any other boat, but I was looking in the wrong direction. Herbert pointed again . . . not in the direction from where the *Hamburg* was approaching, nor in the direction from which we had just come.

The Hamburg

Hiding among a bed of reeds

He was pointing to the land of my childhood. A boat had left the shore and was
heading out across the water, straight toward
us.

"What is it?" I asked nervously.

"I don't know," replied Herbert.

It was Magwitch who gave the answer.
"She's a four-man cutter," he announced. "A
river police boat for sure."

Now we all turned to look at the *Hamburg*.
She was speeding down towards us, her paddles
beating like thunder. Then we looked again at
the cutter.

"Turn back!" I shouted. "She'll be on us
before the *Hamburg* gets here!"

"No!" yelled Herbert. "We'll make it yet!"

The three vessels were all on a course to
meet. Yard by yard, the *Hamburg* came closer.
So did the police cutter. Now we could see that
there were nine men in that boat.

Four men were rowing. Behind them were
four other men in uniform. And at the front,
all alone, was a man pointing towards us and
urging on the oarsmen.

"Get ready," said Herbert, as we turned our
boat onto a parallel course to the approaching
Hamburg.

"Farewell, Magwitch," I shouted, as the time for our parting arrived. "We'll meet again soon."

"Aye, dear boy, we will," he replied.

"Have you got your money?" I asked.

"Enough to bribe the skipper of the *Hamburg* to take me to Germany," laughed old Magwitch.

The ship was now close enough to see an anchor rope hanging down from behind the paddles.

"Pull yourself aboard on the rope as we come alongside," I shouted.

The police cutter was trying to make speed and cut in front of the *Hamburg* before she reached us. I clearly saw the man standing up at the front of the boat now. It was Orlick. He must have escaped from his bonds and alerted the police.

I saw one uniformed man at the back of the cutter stand up. "Move over! Move over!" he shouted. "You have an escaped convict aboard. Move over! Stop rowing!"

It was too late. The *Hamburg* was on us. I heard the skipper of the *Hamburg* call out, "Stop the paddles!"

The sudden loss of power sent the ship

"We'll make it yet!"

deeper into the water, producing a huge surging wave that raced toward both us and the police boat . . .

Chapter 24
Disaster!

The surging wave hit us first. Magwitch, who had been standing up ready to leap aboard the *Hamburg*, was thrown overboard. He vanished beneath the paddles. The wave continued on to hit the police cutter. I heard Orlick scream before he too tumbled into the water, and vanished beneath the surface.

I stripped off my coat and shirt, and dived in to try and find Magwitch. He resurfaced on the other side of the paddles, which were still slowly turning. They had clearly swept him under the water and out again.

I swam over to him and pulled him back to our boat, and Herbert dragged him inside. The poor man had been badly injured by the paddles. There were cuts all over him, and he could hardly breathe for a crushing wound to his chest.

The next thing I knew, a police sergeant had leapt aboard and locked manacles on Magwitch's wrists and ankles.

Diving in to try to find Magwitch

There was no immediate sign of Orlick. The sea and the paddles must have claimed him. A few moments later, his body floated to the surface.

Herbert and I rowed slowly and sadly to the shore, under escort from the police cutter.

Magwitch, now unconscious, was put aboard the cutter. I asked to be allowed to accompany him to whatever destination they intended. It was agreed.

I held Magwitch in my arms, trying to keep him warm. It was strange to think that once

I held Magwitch in my arms.

I could not bear to be close to him. But now all had changed. I truly did think of him as a kindly father figure. I realized there was a lot more good than bad in Magwitch.

His breathing became worse as we neared London. He groaned as he recovered consciousness at last. He was in great pain.

"I'm sorry it's come to this," I said. "I wish now you hadn't come back. I know you did it for my sake. But you shouldn't have risked it."

"Dear boy," he murmured, "I was quite happy to take my chances. I've seen my boy, and he can certainly be a young gentleman now without me being around. Now lookee here, boy, it's best you pretend we're not too friendly in front of these men. It's not right for a gentleman and a criminal to be so close."

I smiled and promised I would never forget him, and would visit him every day in prison. It was a promise I intended to keep this time. Magwitch and Joe had both taught me lessons in friendship. "I'll never stir from your side," I said. "I'll be as true to you as you have been to me."

I didn't tell him that my days as a gentleman must be numbered. His next resting place was Newgate Prison. From that moment on, all his assets would be confiscated and become the property of the King. If I was to be a gentleman, I would be a very poor one now.

After Magwitch was taken away, I hurried around to see Mr. Jaggers and tell him what had happened.

He looked at me grimly. "I fear there is nothing I can do to save him now," he said. "There is only one penalty for a convict escaping from Australia."

Magwitch lay in prison for some weeks. He still couldn't breathe properly and his wounds failed to heal. I saw him every day, thanks to Jaggers and Wemmick, using their influence with the prison guards.

Magwitch seemed a resigned and tired man now, and he had to be carried into the courtroom when his case was finally heard. Jaggers, Wemmick, and I all spoke on his behalf, and told the judge how he had helped me to become a gentleman. The judge was a kindly man, but even he had no power to avoid the only sentence available.

Magwitch would have to hang.

In the days that followed I wrote to many government officials, asking for mercy. There was none to be had.

Disaster!

I saw Magwitch for the last time late one afternoon. The last rays of the sun were just creeping into his cell through the barred window.

"Well, Pip," he said, weakly. "Things have come to a pretty pass, eh? I thankee for not deserting me. You've been a true friend. To have you as a friend is the best thing that ever happened in my life."

He lay back on his bed, breathing with great difficulty.

"Are you in pain?" I asked.

"I don't complain of any, my dear boy, my young gentleman," he whispered.

"You never do complain, do you," I replied.

There was no answer. He had spoken his last words.

At that moment, the Prison Governor came in. He saw that my friend must be dying. I asked if I could stay for a while. He nodded kindly and left us alone.

"You know, old friend," I said, holding Magwitch's hand. "I have something I must tell you."

I felt a gentle pressure on my hand.

"You had a child once, didn't you?" I asked quietly. "A child you must have loved and lost?"

Magwitch had spoken his last words.

Disaster!

Again, I felt pressure on my hand, as if he was answering, "Yes."

"Well," I said, "she's still alive and has found powerful friends. She has become a beautiful and wealthy lady. And do you know, I love her."

With one last effort, he raised my hands to his lips and kissed them. Then, slowly, his head sank onto his chest.

I think he died happy that, despite his roguish ways, his biggest achievement in life had been to produce both a lady and a gentleman.

Chapter 25
A Great Surprise

A few days later, I went down with a terrible fever. I was woken from my sickbed soon after by a knock at the door. I opened it to find two men. They had come to inform me that I would shortly be arrested and thrown into the debtors' prison, if I didn't clear what I now owed.

I had no money left now and had run up some large debts. There was nothing I could do, in my state. I retired to my sickbed and rather hoped to join Magwitch in heaven.

The next time I awoke, I thought that's where I had gone. I had been dreaming that dear Joe was wiping my fevered brow, but it was no dream. The news of my illness, and my debts, had been sent by Wemmick to Joe. He had immediately traveled up to London to care for me.

Joe stayed with me for two weeks as I drifted in and out of the fever. Gradually I got

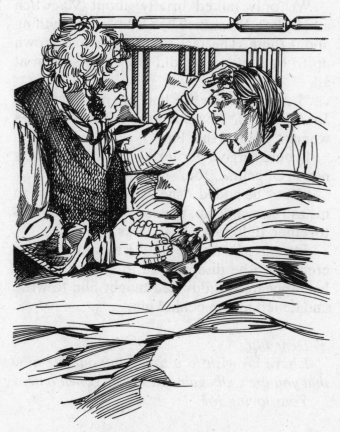

Wiping my fevered brow

better, and he took me out for long walks in the country. It was now early summer and the smell of sweet blossom filled the air.

We only talked briefly about Magwitch and Orlick. Wemmick had told Joe everything about them. The fact that Orlick had grown up to be a murderer did not surprise him at all.

"I always knew he had hit my dear Mrs. Joe," he said. "Now she were a fine figure of a woman, weren't she, Pip?"

I could forgive her for all her shortcomings now. "Of course, Joe," I replied.

"Yet," he added, "she was never as close to me as I was, and am, to you. We had such larks together, didn't we? Such larks, eh, Pip?"

Joe stayed with me until I was fully recovered. Then he disappeared as suddenly as he had appeared. Biddy had taught him to write and he left a note behind him.

Dear Pip,
I have no wish to intrude on your life now that you are well again. So I have gone home.
Your loving Joe

Enclosed with the note was a receipt. He had paid off the debts that would have delivered me into jail by the end of the week. I decided it was time I went home.

There were no more comfortable coaches for me. A few days later, I hitched a ride on the back of an old farm wagon. On that wagon, I started to think of Biddy. Perhaps I had been wrong all along. Perhaps I should have married her, even though I knew in my heart of hearts that it was Estella I loved.

It took me the whole day to reach the village. It was just my luck that old Pumblechook saw my humble arrival that evening. He was well aware that my fortunes had changed.

"Well, well," he said. "I am sorry to see you in such poor circumstances. Yet, it's nothing unexpected. I thought you would be crawling home sooner than this, you ungrateful boy. And after all the things I did for you!"

I ignored the bumbling fool and hurried on to the forge. The sun was just setting over the marsh. I don't think I had ever seen it looking so beautiful. The sky was full of singing larks.

I looked inside the forge because Joe would normally be working late there. But there was no sound of hammer on anvil; no gleam of fire,

163

Old Pumblechook saw my humble arrival.

no stream of sparks or roar of bellows.

Then I heard laughter and looked at the house. There were pretty white curtains flutering at the windows and a coat of fresh white paint on the door.

I walked slowly into the house and what a surprise met my eyes! Joe and Biddy were arm in arm. He was in his smart suit and Biddy was wearing a wedding dress.

At first Biddy gave a cry, as if she had seen a ghost. And then she began to weep.

"Oh dear Pip," she sobbed. "How good to see you."

"Yes, old chap," added Joe. "We always wanted you join us on our special day. But we thought you wouldn't be well enough to come."

I had never seen such a happy couple. They had only been married a few hours!

Chapter 26
A New Start

"You've made our marriage day complete," said Joe.

"Yes," added Biddy, giving me a huge hug.

And as for me, I truly was happy for them. My earlier thoughts about perhaps marrying Biddy were just childish memories. Biddy and I would always be best as just great friends.

"Biddy," I said, "you now have the best husband in the whole world . . . and Joe, you have the best wife. I hope you will make each other as happy as you surely deserve."

They couldn't stop hugging me and saying how happy they were to see me. But I had more to say.

"I want to thank you for all you both did for me in times past," I began, "and I apologize that I have so badly repaid your kindnesses. I shall be leaving tomorrow, to set out to earn the money that Joe paid to save me from the debtors' prison. Yet, I could earn ten fortunes

They couldn't stop hugging me.

and still wouldn't have enough to pay you back for all you have done for me. Can you forgive me for forgetting you when I came into my fortune?"

"You have nothing to be forgiven for," said Joe. "We were friends when we were young, and we are still friends. So nothing's changed, has it?"

"And so say I," added Biddy.

That night we had a wonderful wedding feast.

During the evening I said how I hoped they would have children. "Maybe one day I will visit and find a little fellow like me, sitting in the chimney corner," I said. "May he remind you of me. You can tell him how much I loved you, and also tell him how there was a time when I didn't deserve your love."

"I shall tell him no such thing," said Joe. "Nor will Biddy. You always deserved our love."

The next morning, they waved goodbye to me again. Another farm cart was to take me back to London.

I passed old Pumblechook on the way out of the village. I saw him stick his nose in the air when he saw the muddy cart I was on. I stuck my nose in air too, and proudly journeyed on to London.

When I got back to London, I found that Herbert had returned. And he had a plan for me. He wanted me to join him and Clarriker in their shipping company. The plan was for me to go abroad immediately.

"I know your secret," said Herbert. "I know now that it was you that paid to put me in partnership with Clarriker. So, now it's my turn to help you."

How could I refuse him? It all worked out well too. Herbert and his lovely new wife, Clara, let me share their house.

We didn't make a fortune, but we made a good living. I paid back the money I owed to Joe and I wrote to him and Biddy every week.

***

It was eleven years before I returned to England. I went straight to see my greatest friends. It was Christmas Eve when I finally arrived at my birthplace on the Kent marshes.

I opened the kitchen door of the old house

It was eleven years before I returned.

and saw a young boy, sitting in the chimney corner, perched on my own little stool. Joe, sitting in his usual chair with Biddy beside him, saw me enter.

Before he even greeted me, Joe looked at the little boy and then back to me. "We called him Pip after you, dear chap," he said. "We hoped he might grow a little like you, and we think he has."

We had a happy reunion that night and the next day, too. On Christmas morning I took young Pip to the church on the marsh. I sat him on the very tombstone that Magwitch had put me on, and thought about all that had happened to me in my life. Then I visited the graves of my parents and brothers, and my sister, too. Oh, how I wished they could see me now!

That afternoon, Biddy took me for a walk and asked me whether I had married.

"Oh no!" I exclaimed. "I shall be a bachelor all my life."

"Do you still think of *her*?" she asked. "Has your heart forgotten her?"

"Estella had an important place in my life," I said. "But it was a dream that is all gone."

"Are you sure?" asked Biddy.

Biddy knew me better than anyone. Of course, the dream remained. I had always loved Estella, and I had already planned to go and visit the site of Miss Haversham's old house.

Chapter 27
An Extraordinary Meeting

On Christmas night, I walked down to the village. A cold shivery mist rolled in off the marsh as I reached the old house site. It was a desolate spot now, because Miss Haversham's house had been demolished after she died. Only part of the garden remained.

I started to think about Estella. I'd heard that she had not had a happy life. She had married the wealthy rower, Bentley Drummle, but he turned out to be a brutal fellow. He had died in a riding accident after beating a horse half to death. I'd heard no news about her having married again.

It was then that I saw a solitary figure strolling across the garden. It was a woman. She saw me and walked toward me.

It might seem an extraordinary coincidence, yet, to me, it seemed as if it was meant to be.

"Estella!" I cried.

"I am so different now, I wonder you recognized me," she said, coming up to my side.

The freshness of her beauty had gone, but she was lovely still. The biggest change in her was a sad look in those once-proud eyes.

We sat down on a bench to talk.

"Do you often come back here?" I asked.

"No," she replied. "This is the first time for many a year. It is such a sad place for me."

The silvery mist was touched by the first rays of the rising moon. The light showed tears in her eyes.

"I have sold the land and a new house is to be built here," she said. "That's why I am here this evening, to say goodbye to the old place."

As we sat there, she asked me if I still lived abroad. I said that I did.

"I often think of you," she said.

"Do you?" I asked.

"Of late, very often," she replied. "Now I see what I didn't see in you when we were young. I married Bentley Drummle out of spite for all the young men who pursued me. But remember what I said to you . . . that you were the only one who I wasn't trying to trap. You were different."

"You have always held a special place in my heart," I said.

"Estella!"

Estella told me she was living in London and would welcome me, if I wished to visit her.

"Tell me, Pip, tell me that we are still friends," she said, before she had to go.

"We are still friends," I replied, taking her hands in mine. "And we shall always be."

"I hope so," said Estella, disappearing into the shadows. "And I hope that we shall meet again very soon."

I watched her go, but this time quite happily. I knew that I would see her again, and that we

The light showed tears in her eyes.

would never be parted. I had great expectations and suddenly, the future looked very bright indeed.

The End